BEARHEAD

A Russian Folktale adapted
by ERIC A. KIMMEL

BEARHEAD

with illustrations by
CHARLES MIKOLAYCAK

Holiday House/New York

Library of Congress Cataloging-in-Publication Data
Kimmel, Eric A.
Bearhead : a Russian folktale / by Eric A. Kimmel :
illustrations by Charles Mikolaycak. —1st ed.
p.   cm.
Summary: Bearhead succeeds in outwitting the witch
Madame Hexaba and a frog-headed goblin.
ISBN 0-8234-0902-3
[1. Fairy tales.   2. Folklore—Soviet Union.]
I. Mikolaycak, Charles, ill.   II. Title.
PZ8.K527Be   1991   91-55026   CIP   AC
398.2—dc20
[E]
ISBN 0-8234-1302-0 (pbk.)

Designed by Charles Mikolaycak

The illustrations were done in
watercolor and colored pencil on Diazo prints.

Thanks to Niel, Hero and Fantomas.   C.M.

To Sean, Mark, and Laura   E.A.K.

To patient Margery   C.M.

AUTHOR'S NOTE

Bearhead is adapted from one of my favorite Russian tales, *Ivanko the Bear's Son*. In that story, the hero has the body of a bear and the head of a human being. I thought he'd be more interesting in a man's body with a bear's head; thus the name *Bearhead*. Madame Hexaba is also a personal insertion. (Ivanko's opponent in the original tale is his stepfather.) Her name is a combination of *hexe*, the German word for witch, and *aba*, a Ukrainian family name ending.

This story is one of my favorites because Bearhead, like many small children, interprets things literally, and one never knows if he's sly or just plain foolish.

Eric A. Kimmel

One day in early spring a woman went to the forest to gather mushrooms. As she was filling her basket, she heard a cry from beneath a pile of dead leaves. She brushed the leaves aside and found a baby. But not an ordinary one. From its neck up it had the eyes, ears, and muzzle of a bear cub. The woman had no children of her own, so she wrapped the baby in her shawl, put it in her basket, and took it home.

Her husband shook his head when he saw the strange foundling. "This baby must belong to the bear folk," he told his wife. "I think you should put it back where you found it."

His wife refused. However strange this baby was, she meant to keep it. But he needed a name, so she gave him the first one that came to mind: **BEARHEAD**

Years went by. Bearhead grew up. He not only looked like a bear; he was as big as a bear and just as strong. His parents grew used to his odd appearance. After a while they ceased to notice it. They loved Bearhead as if he were their own child. And Bearhead loved them. He tried his best to be an obedient son, always doing exactly what he was told.

One day Bearhead's father received a letter from Madame Hexaba summoning him to be her servant. Bearhead's father shook with fear. Madame Hexaba was a witch who owned all the lands around. No one who entered her palace ever returned. "Father, do not worry," Bearhead said. "I will go in your place. I am not afraid of Madame Hexaba. After all, I can do the work of ten strong men."

Bearhead kissed his parents good-bye and walked all the way to Madame Hexaba's palace. He arrived just as the old witch was finishing her supper.

"Who are you? What are you doing here?" she shrieked when she saw him.

Bearhead bowed low. "My name is Bearhead," he said. "My father sent me to be your new servant."

Madame Hexaba laughed. "Servant? You? Creatures like you belong in a cage, not a palace! However, I am a kind witch, so I will give you a chance to prove yourself. Show me how quickly you can clear away this table."

"Quicker than you think," Bearhead said. He picked up the whole table, platters and all, and flung it out the window. It fell in the courtyard with a crash.

"What is the matter with you? Have you lost your wits?" Madame Hexaba screeched. "I didn't want you to throw the table out the window! I meant put away the dishes!"

Bearhead shrugged. "You should say what you mean."

"That's no excuse," Madame Hexaba replied. "Apologize at once!"

"I'm sorry I threw your table out the window," said Bearhead.

"That's not good enough! Show me you're really sorry. Kiss my feet!"

"Whatever you wish." Bearhead grabbed Madame Hexaba by the ankles, jerked her upside down, and planted big kisses on her toes.

"Let me go! Let me go at once!" Madame Hexaba shrieked.

Bearhead let her go. Madame Hexaba landed on her head. She lay on the floor, moaning.

"Poor old witch," said Bearhead. "Did you hurt yourself? Shall I kiss your feet again?"

"No, no," Madame Hexaba groaned. "You are too dangerous to have in the house. I must find work for you outside."

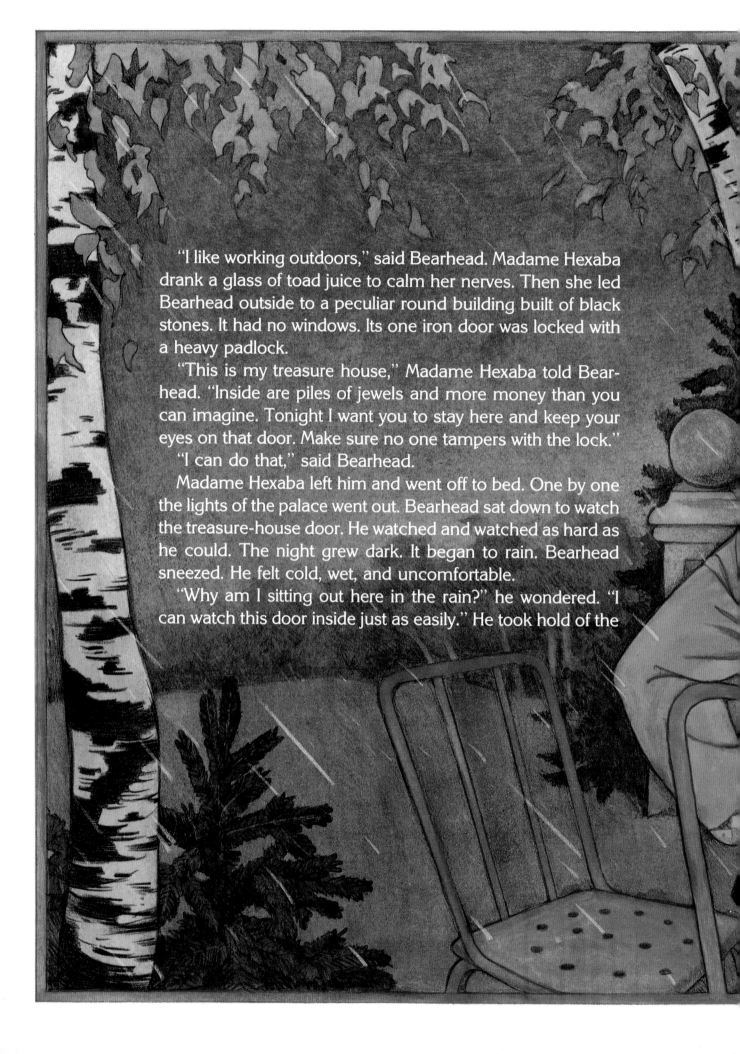

"I like working outdoors," said Bearhead. Madame Hexaba drank a glass of toad juice to calm her nerves. Then she led Bearhead outside to a peculiar round building built of black stones. It had no windows. Its one iron door was locked with a heavy padlock.

"This is my treasure house," Madame Hexaba told Bearhead. "Inside are piles of jewels and more money than you can imagine. Tonight I want you to stay here and keep your eyes on that door. Make sure no one tampers with the lock."

"I can do that," said Bearhead.

Madame Hexaba left him and went off to bed. One by one the lights of the palace went out. Bearhead sat down to watch the treasure-house door. He watched and watched as hard as he could. The night grew dark. It began to rain. Bearhead sneezed. He felt cold, wet, and uncomfortable.

"Why am I sitting out here in the rain?" he wondered. "I can watch this door inside just as easily." He took hold of the

heavy iron door and ripped it off its hinges, padlock and all. Then he lifted it onto his back and carried it inside.

Later that night a band of robbers rode by. Finding the witch's treasure house wide open, they wasted no time in making off with every bit of her treasure.

The next morning, when Madame Hexaba found her treasure gone, she let out a shriek. "What did you do?" she screamed at Bearhead. "I told you to guard my treasure house!"

"You did not," Bearhead replied. "You told me to keep my eyes on the door and make sure no one tampered with the lock. I did that. The door is in the kitchen, safe and sound. So is the lock. I watched them all night. No one tampered with either one."

Madame Hexaba fell to the ground. "Ay, ay, ay! What will I do with this Bearhead? He will be the ruin of me." She rolled in the dirt, moaning and groaning. But then she got up, brushed off her skirts, and said in a voice dripping with honey,

"Bearhead dear, I have a special job for you. On the other side of the forest is a lake, and in that lake lives a goblin. He hasn't paid rent in a hundred years. I want you to go to that lake and make that goblin pay what he owes."

"A hundred years is a lot of rent. How will I carry all that money?"

"Take a wagon with you," Madame Hexaba told him. "You're strong. You can pull a wagon by yourself. You don't need a horse."

Bearhead found a wagon. Pulling it behind him, he started off down the road. Madame Hexaba waited until he was out of sight. Then she laughed so hard her teeth cracked.

"This will pay that wicked Bearhead back for what he did to me. That goblin is a fearsome creature. Even I am afraid of him! No one who goes near that lake ever returns."

But Bearhead knew nothing of this. As he walked through the forest, pulling the wagon behind, he noticed something fluttering in a tree. It was a wren caught in a snare. Bearhead freed the tiny creature and put it in his pocket. Taking hold of the wagon once more, he continued on his way.

The road through the forest ended at a rocky beach where nothing grew except the weathered stumps of long-dead trees. As Bearhead approached the lake he noticed that the birds had stopped singing. No insects hummed. The only sound was the slap-slap-slap of waves against the shore.

Bearhead went down to the lake. Gathering up the biggest rocks he could find, he threw them one by one into the water.

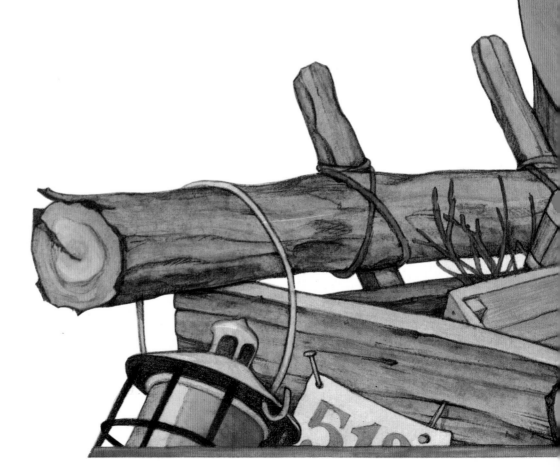

All at once the lake began to bubble and boil. Then the goblin appeared. He had long scaly arms, an eel's winding body, and the head of a giant frog. On top of his head he wore a tall green hat. "Hey! Who's throwing rocks through my window?" the goblin snarled.

"I am," Bearhead said, folding his arms across his chest and looking the goblin in the eye.

"You?" The goblin stared at Bearhead, but instead of flying into a rage, he only laughed. "Well, aren't you a sight! I know I look strange, but you take the prize. We must be cousins. What can I do for you, cousin?"

"Madame Hexaba sent me," Bearhead told the goblin. "She wants you to pay the rent you owe."

"Ha!" the goblin sneered. "That old witch can whistle for her rent. But since we're cousins, I'll make you a deal. Let's see who can throw a rock the farthest. If you win, you can have anything you want. But if you lose, then down below the lake you come to live with me."

"That's fair," Bearhead agreed.

The goblin reached out and picked up a rock as big as Bearhead's wagon. He threw it across the lake. Bearhead watched it splash on the other side.

"Good throw, cousin," Bearhead said. "But your rock splashed into the lake. Mine won't. It will keep on going. Watch!" He reached into his pocket and cupped the little wren in his hand. "Fly, bird, fly," he whispered as he threw it into the air. The wren stretched out its wings, flew across the lake, and disappeared into the trees.

The goblin frowned. "You're a tricky fellow. Your rock was a lot smaller than I expected. All the same, you won. Tell me what you want."

"Not much," said Bearhead. "Fill my wagon with gold. And give me your hat. I've taken a fancy to it."

The goblin didn't mind the gold, but he hated losing his hat. Even so, he kept his word. Bearhead started back toward Madame Hexaba's palace with a wagon full of gold and the goblin's tall green hat pulled down over his ears.

Madame Hexaba was in the tower room watering her poison ivy when she saw the tall green hat coming over the hill. "The goblin! He's coming to get me!" the old witch yelped. She ran all over the palace, pulling in shutters and bolting doors. Finally she threw herself under the bed and lay there trembling.

Bearhead stopped at Madame Hexaba's front door. To his surprise he found the palace locked and barred. He knocked. "I'm here. Open the door. I brought your rent money."

Madame Hexaba peeped out from under the bed. When she saw the tall green hat framed in the window, she thought it was the goblin for sure.

"Go away! Go away!" she whimpered.

"But what shall I do with the money?" Bearhead asked her.

"Keep it!" Madame Hexaba cried.

"Whatever you say," said Bearhead. He started off toward his parent's house, pulling the wagon behind him.

His mother and father were overjoyed to see him. When they saw all the gold he brought with him, their delight knew no bounds. Bearhead was happy too. Yet at the same time he could not help feeling sad.

"I can only stay a short time," he told his parents. "Then I must be on my way."

"To where?" they asked him. "Isn't this your home?"

"No, not any longer. Tomorrow I must return to the forest. A voice inside my heart speaks to me. It says the time has come for me to find my own people, to make a new life for myself with them."

Bearhead's mother began to cry. "Surely you will come back some day."

"I do not know, Mother," Bearhead said. "But watch for me when the acorns fall and the mushrooms are ready to be gathered. Perhaps I will come again."

And indeed, one day he did come again.
But that is another story.